A new SCARETOWN book is released every month.
Sign up to the mailing list at
www.scaretownbooks.com for access to exclusive
deals on the newest releases.

Join the conversation at
www.twitter.com/scaretownbooks

For my mum and dad.

DEAD MAN'S WOODS

L.A. Drake

CHAPTER ONE

WE'D BEEN LIVING in our new neighbourhood for two months before I plucked up the courage to enter Dead Man's Woods. The school holidays had started and the summer heat made the house unbearable. Sweat dripped from my face as I chucked my puzzle book to the side and hauled myself towards the front door.

"Cassie!" Arj shouted when I opened it. He stood on the doorstep with a stupid grin.

"What is it, Arj?" I said, feeling a wave of humid air slap me across the face.

"Come with me, I've got something to show you."

"But, it's so hot. I just want to stay inside and melt," I said, wiping my brow again.

"Come on!" he pleaded. "You'll like it, I promise."

Arj was the only person I'd spoken to in my new school. He wasn't the coolest or smartest kid in class, but he was always kind and made me feel welcome when everything was scary and new. On my first day, he made space at his desk and invited me to join him. We'd hung out at every break time since.

"OK," I said. "But it better be worth it!"

I slipped into my trainers but, just as I was stepping out the door, I heard a booming voice shouting from the other room.

"WHERE DO YOU THINK YOU'RE GOING, YOUNG LADY?" my mum called.

"Out!" I said, simply.

"Not without your little brother, you're not,' she said, more calmly. "Look at him, he needs a good airing."

I peeked back through the door to see my brother Daniel slouched on the sofa, playing on his phone.

"Come on, get up!" Mum said, grabbing him by the arm and hoisting him into the air. "It'll do you good to get out the house for a bit."

"But, Mum!" Daniel moaned, "I don't wanna hang out with Cassie and her boyfriend!"

"Arj isn't my boyfriend!" I said sharply. I could feel the blood rushing to my cheeks.

"Nonsense," Mum continued. "She's your sister. You'll have fun together. This isn't a discussion. And while you're at it, you can take Smoke for a walk."

Smoke was our dog. A 3-year-old, jet-black Doberman that would scare the life out of almost everyone who saw her but, in reality, was the softest, most cuddly puppy-dog you could ever meet. Mum ushered us out the door and, together with Arj, we stumbled forward into the street.

"You can hang out with us, but don't be annoying!" I said, turning to face Daniel. He shrugged and looked down at his phone again.

"Hi, Daniel!" Arj said with a smile. "Hi, Smoke!"

Smoke wagged her stumpy tail enthusiastically. Daniel grunted.

"That means hello in Daniel-speak," I said.

"I didn't know you were bilingual," Arj said, before giggling to himself as if he'd said something funny. I smiled and nodded.

"What was it you wanted to show me, anyway?"

"You're gonna love it!" Arj said as we started walking. Daniel trailed along behind, face down, engrossed in his phone.

"Where is it?" I asked. "What is it?"

"Up there," Arj replied with a nod that made me stop in my tracks.

"In …Dead Man's Woods?" I asked, trying to sound casual. I tugged at my t-shirt to let the air flow more freely. The sun was beating down and the air was still.

I lifted my hand to shield my eyes. Through a gap in a row of houses we could see a line of tall, dark green trees. Dead Man's Woods, as it was known to all the kids at school, was a dense and overgrown area on the very edge of town. Nobody had ever ventured into Dead Man's Woods. One time, when a football landed in the trees, the players decided to buy a new one rather than go into the spooky undergrowth.

"We're going to Dead Man's Woods!?" Daniel said, looking up from his phone for the first time.

"No, of course not! It's just next to it. We won't go in, I promise!" Arj replied as we entered an alleyway between two sets of houses.

It wasn't until too late that I realised, some promises are made to be broken.

CHAPTER TWO

WE MOVED FROM the paved street to the muddy patch of ground that separated the town from Dead Man's Woods. We stopped and took a minute to look at the trees that were now looming tall in front of us. They seemed eerily still. The branches barely swayed, the leaves hardly fluttered. The whole place looked as if it was frozen in time.

The bark was cracked and flaking. The leaves were brown and yellow and an invisible wind whistled as it passed through the pitch-black interior. It was a beautiful day with bright blue skies but in Dead Man's Woods it could've been winter. No light penetrated the leafy canopy and it was impossible to see past the first line of trees. I shivered. Smoke whimpered. I scratched her ears and told her she was a good girl.

"Come on," Arj said, patting me on the shoulder. "This way."

We turned right, leaving the woods behind. As we passed through some low bushes and skipped lightly through a patch of stinging nettles, I heard a voice from behind us.

"That's the ugliest dog I've ever seen." It was Luca from school. He stood astride his BMX with a dumb smirk plastered across his freckly face. "He must be related to you, Arj!" He added, his smirk erupting into a throaty laugh. His boney shoulders jerked up and down.

Arj looked at his feet. Smoke barked. I tugged on the lead.

"Ooh, quick Arj, your mother is calling you!" Luca said, causing himself to laugh maniacally again.

"Shut up!" I said. I was in no mood to argue. It was too hot and too early.

"Does your girlfriend fight all your battles for you, Arjy?" Luca continued. His tight lips stretched into a smile.

"I mean it, Luca!" I said.

"Ooh, she means it! I'm really scared now!" he said, still laughing.

I lunged forward. Smoke lunged with me and let out a fierce growl, but Luca was too quick. In a flash, he'd spun his bike around and started pedalling hard. In my haste, I tripped and fell. I landed in the stinging nettles. I looked up to see Luca speeding off into the distance, his laugh hanging in the air as his skinny silhouette disappeared from sight.

Suddenly, I felt two sets of hands grab me by the shoulders.

"Who the heck was that?" Daniel said, helping me to my feet as Arj flicked the mud from my hair.

"That was Luca Barnes," I said, regaining my composure and applying pressure to my stings. "He's

11

in my form at school. He's all mouth, but you shouldn't let him speak to you like that, Arj."

"I know," he said, looking at his shoes again. "I'm sorry."

Smoke was milling about between my legs, still confused and excited, when Daniel's face went pale and he stared into the distance.

"What on earth is *that!*?" he said, shakily pointing towards Dead Man's Woods.

CHAPTER THREE

"YOU FOUND IT!" Arj said. "That's what I wanted to show you!"

Smoke bounded forward and started sniffing expectantly at a patch of long grass. Her stumpy tail swung back and forth like a metronome.

"What is it!?" I asked, peering over Smoke's shoulders at a brown mass a few metres away.

"It's a deer!" Arj replied. "Well, it used to be."

I called Smoke off as we approached the animal. It was dead. The lower half of its body had been ripped in two and flesh and bone stuck out at odd angles. A putrid smell grew in strength as we got closer.

"That's disgusting!" I said, holding my nose.

"It's so cool!" Daniel said, brushing past me to get a better look.

"I know, right?" Arj replied. "Look at this."

He picked up a stick and poked the deer's backside. A slow ooze of black blood squidged out, followed by a cascade of maggots and flies.

"Eww!" I said, stepping back.

"Sick!" Daniel purred, grinning like a Cheshire cat. "Let me have a go!"

"*This* is what you wanted to show me, Arj?" I said, bending low to scratch the stings on my knees.

"Yeah, you don't know her very well, do you?" Daniel added with a laugh.

"No! I knew you'd hate this," Arj replied quickly. "But, don't you think it's strange? It's like something took a bite out it. Something *huge*."

Arj was right. This wasn't a normal dead deer. It had been torn apart by something ferocious.

"I know you love puzzles. I thought you might like investigating this," he added softly. I took a second to consider what he'd said and then stepped forward to take another look at the animal. The skin had been torn roughly and bright white bits of bone shone out between swathes of purple flesh.

"It is strange…" I confessed. "What do you think could've done this?"

"A bear!" Daniel said suddenly.

Arj and I looked at him, then at each other, then burst out laughing.

"There are no bears here, Daniel," I said. "Nor tigers or wolves or vampires!"

I laughed again but, when I turned back to Arj, his smile had fallen and his face was ashen grey.

"What's wrong?" I asked.

"There is one thing that it could be…" he said slowly. "But you'll probably think it's stupid."

"What is it?" Daniel said. "We won't laugh, will we Cassie?"

I shook my head and looked seriously at Arj. Something was bothering him. I swatted a fly away from my face.

"It could be the zombies in Dead Man's Woods," he said. He wasn't joking. His face was stern and he looked terrified. He peered up at us with bright, wide eyes.

Daniel's jaw dropped. We'd all heard the rumours and stories of strange things living in the woods. We looked at Arj again and …burst out laughing.

"Come on, Arj! You don't seriously believe that do you?" I said, incredulously.

"Mate, it's just a load of kid's stories," Daniel added.

Arj didn't laugh. He just turned and started walking slowly home. As I watched him disappear around the corner, I saw something out the corner of my eye. I turned to look across the muddy patch of land, but nothing was there.

Then, I heard something.

I span around and saw something huge emerging from the bush.

CHAPTER FOUR

I SCREAMED AT the top of my lungs as the thing leapt towards us. I stumbled and fell backwards into the dirt. Daniel scrambled back next to me. The thing from the bushed lunged at us with a jagged saw blade in its hands. I started to scream again before I realised, it was Luca Barnes. He was standing over us and the sun was framing his lanky body. He arched his back and laughed loudly.

"I got you good!" he said, grinning like a madman and lowering the saw to his side. I brushed myself down, jumped to my feet pushed him hard in the chest with both hands.

"Woah, calm down Cassie! It's just a joke," he said, taking a step back.

"Well, it's not funny!" I shot back. I could feel my pulse racing. He got me good and I'd lost my temper. "Why the heck have you got a saw?"

"Alright, alright. I'm sorry. Geez!" he said, looking to Daniel for help. "I was on my way to help my dad cut a tree in the garden. The branches have got so long they're starting to fall over the neighbour's fence. I thought it would be funny to scare you at the same time."

He shrugged as if jumping out a bush with a saw in your hands was the most normal thing in the world. I looked at Daniel. His brow was furrowed and his mouth was hanging open. He looked as confused as I felt.

"Why do you always do these things, Luca? What's your problem?" I said angrily, before turning to walk away. I have a short fuse and my dad always says to remove myself from a situation if I'm getting too worked up. I stomped back the way we'd come and heard Daniel jogging behind.

"That guy is so annoying," I said to Daniel when he'd eventually caught up.

"Cassie… Did you see his face?" he said. "That was hilarious. He didn't know what to do."

I looked at Daniel. I was still fuming and I didn't want to laugh, but Daniel was grinning from ear to ear.

"Yeah…" A slight smile appeared on my lips.

"He thought you were completely crazy!" Daniel said, and this time we both laughed.

"I guess I did get a bit angry, didn't I?"

"A bit? He was scared for his life!"

We laughed all the way back to the house with Daniel doing impressions of Luca's terrified face. When we got home, Mum was waiting for us in the kitchen and Dad was sitting in the living room watching TV.

"What have you been doing?" Mum asked, looking down at our muddy clothes.

"I leave you for ten minutes and you come back filthy!"

"We're fine, Mum," I said.

"Yeah. We just saw this really cool dead deer over by Dead Man's Woods..." Daniel added before I nudged him in the side to make him stop.

"Dead Man's Woods!?" Mum asked in a high-pitch voice.

"I thought you'd be more worried about the deer, honestly," I said. Daniel laughed, as Dad entered the kitchen.

"Did you go into the woods?" he asked, hastily.

"No," I replied. "We just went near. Arj wanted to show us..."

"Cassie. Be honest. Did you go into Dead Man's Woods?" he asked again. Mum was stood next to him looking serious.

"No!" I said again.

Suddenly, their demeanours changed and their faces softened.

"Good. Just checking." Mum said, forcing a smile. "Now, go upstairs and get changed out of those muddy clothes."

We did as we were told and headed towards our bedrooms. With his hand on the door-handle, Daniel turned to me.

"Why do you think they were so worried about us going to the woods?" He asked.

"I don't know, but I've never seen Dad act like that. It was like he was scared."

"Scared of what?"

"I don't know, but I've got a feeling we're gonna find out."

CHAPTER FIVE

THE EVENING WENT by quickly and I was soon ready for bed. The sun had gone down but its heat remained and I lay awake, tossing and turning to get comfortable. The windows were wide open and my desk fan circulated the warm night air around the room. The bedsheet clung to my skin and I could feel it slowly peel away as I rolled over. Beads of sweat formed on my forehead and I yearned for water.

Eventually, I sat up. The heat was still unbearable and I couldn't sleep. I swung my legs off the bed and grabbed a glass from the bedside table. I gulped down as much as I could and stood up to walk to the window. The creaking floor echoed around the room.

The rest of the house was almost silent. Daniel had gone to bed and was probably fast asleep. He slept like a log. My parents were still downstairs. They always put the TV on low but tonight it was drowned out by the whirring of my fan on its highest setting. The mechanical blades circulated warm air over my body.

I leaned against the window sill and tried to get some fresh air. I stuck my head through the opening, but the outside was just as muggy as inside. I felt trapped, unable to escape the oppressive heat. I sighed deeply and leant on my elbows.

The street was quiet and dark. A little light peered out from behind the curtains in a stranger's house. In the distance, Dead Man's Woods were backlit by a waxing moon. The tall trees stood faintly in front of the night sky, a mass of greys and blacks.

As I looked closer, I could make out the individual tree trunks at the entrance to the woods. Until now, I'd not appreciated how close they were to my house. I could see the natural pathways that led in and out of the tree line. Grey holes leading to pitch black. Darkness leading to darkness. I squinted and leant further out the window for a better look.

That's when I saw it.

I saw something move. Something tall and slender. It was like a person but, even from this distance and in this light, I could tell it wasn't human. It was something *different.* It moved slowly, dragging its limbs as if they were a burden. As if every movement was a struggle. As I watched, it seemed to slowly increase its speed. Each laboured step was a little quicker than the last until, eventually, it broke out into a full sprint. Its arms and legs flailed wildly as if it had no control over where or when they bent.

It disappeared into the depth of the woods but reappeared half a second later. It crashed into a tree but kept running as if it didn't even notice. *What was it doing?* It twisted and turned and then, suddenly, it stopped.

Slowly and deliberately, the thing in the woods turned its ugly head and looked directly at me.

CHAPTER SIX

I SCREAMED, TOOK a step back and ran from the room. I crashed through my door and knocked desperately on Daniel's. The hard wood thudded and groaned under my fists.

"What is it, Cass?" he asked, blearily wiping his eyes. His hair was smeared across his head and the imprints from his pillow still marked his cheek.

I grabbed him by the arm and dragged him to my room.

"Look!" I said, stepping over a pile of clothes and pointing out the window. "Do you see it?"

"What? Dead Man's Woods? Big deal."

"No, look closer!"

"I don't see anything, Cassie. Why are you acting so weird?"

I looked again. I searched the tree line for the *thing* but it was nowhere to be seen. The woods were as still as they had been before. Nothing moved.

"It was right there. I swear…"

"What was? What are you talking about?"

I scoured the view of the woods for any sign of movement but it had gone. Disappeared. I took a step back and slumped down onto my bed. I blinked away the sweat that had dripped into my eye and looked up at my brother.

"Did you have a nightmare? That is …*tragic.*" Daniel said, laughing. I grunted and waved him away. "I thought you'd have grown out of that by now, Cass!"

He shut the door and I laid down, resting my head on the cool side of the pillow. I was sure I'd seen it. Maybe I'd imagined it? Maybe the darkness was playing tricks on me? I was so confused and hot. I rolled over and shut my eyes.

When I opened them again, it was morning. I climbed out of bed and made my way downstairs to find Daniel already at the kitchen table. Dad was sat next to him and Mum was rummaging through a food cupboard just behind. Outside, men worked busily on our new garage.

"Hello, sweetie," Dad said, raising his voice over the noise of hammers hitting nails.

I mumbled hello and slumped down in the nearest chair. My hair looked like a bird's nest and my pyjamas were wrinkled and stretched.

"Rough night?" Mum asked as she closed the cupboard door.

"Just hot," I said. "So hot and sweaty."

"I'll make you a nice cold glass of OJ," Mum said. "Nice and refreshing.'

She liked to use terms like 'OJ' that she'd seen on TV. She started running the tap and fetched a glass from the side.

"No more nightmares, then?" Daniel said with a grin and a sideways glance to our dad.

"Nightmares? What nightmares?" Dad asked, right on queue.

"It's nothing," I said, giving Daniel a quick kick under the table. "I just thought I saw something in the woods."

Dad's face suddenly turned serious.

"Can you believe that, Dad?" Daniel said, finding the whole thing hilarious. "She's a whole year older than me and she's still having nightmares!"

"What kind of thing?" Dad asked. He stood up and shut the kitchen door to close out the sound of drilling from outside. "What woods?"

"It's nothing. Really." I said. "I just saw a person or something in the woods behind the houses. It looked like it was running."

Nobody spoke. Other than Daniel's giggles, the room was silent. Mum had stopped running the tap but still held an empty glass in her hand. Dad looked at her and then back at me.

"I must've had a nightmare," I added, desperately searching for something to say. "Like Daniel said, just a silly dream."

I knew my parents would never laugh at me for having a nightmare, but I didn't think they'd take it quite so seriously. Their faces were pale grey and they looked like they'd seen a ghost. I looked at Daniel. He was still laughing to himself as he ate his cereal. He shook his head as he took another mouthful. A splash of milk dribbled down his chin.

"And…" he said, the word misshapen by mounds of sugary Chocobites. "She ran to my room to tell me about it. As if she still believed it when she was awake!"

He threw his head back and laughed again. I aimed another kick at him under the table and looked at my parents, expecting them to tell us off. However, it looked like they didn't hear a word Daniel had said. Instead, they stared at me. Their faces were stern and worried. Like they were scared.

Like they were terrified.

Like they knew it wasn't a dream at all.

CHAPTER SEVEN

AFTER BREAKFAST, ARJ knocked the door and asked me and Daniel to hang out with him again. I was happy and excited to get out of the house but I was surprised to hear Daniel say he would come too.

"Sure you don't wanna stay in and play video games all day?" I said.

"I'm sure and, besides, someone needs to come and protect you from the monsters in the woods," he shot back with a wink.

"Monsters?" Arj asked with wide, terrified eyes.

"He's just messing around. Don't listen to him," I said, slapping Arj on the back and stepping out into the street with Smoke at my side. "Besides, he's the one that would need protecting."

It was another beautiful day. The sun was shining and the sky was blue and cloudless. It was still early, but I could tell it was going to be blisteringly hot again.

"Let's go see that dead deer!" Daniel suggested brightly, skipping over the rubble the builders had strewn across the front garden.

"Is that the real reason you came with us?" I asked.

"Well, it wasn't for your amazing jokes!"

"Why don't we play run-outs in the field instead?" Arj interjected.

"It's up to you, Cass. Which would you rather?" Daniel reasoned. "Boring old run-outs or the super cool dead deer?"

"As tempting as that stinking animal carcass sounds, I'm gonna have to choose run-outs."

"Fine. I'll see it on the way back," Daniel said.

We walked through the alleyway and emerged into the field behind the houses. Ahead of us, the tall trees of Dead Man's Woods swayed gently in the welcome breeze. The grass was dry and limp. Dust kicked up as we walked.

"Right," I said. "This tree stump will be the home base and the edge of the field is the boundary. Okay?"

"Sounds good to me," said a voice from behind us. As we turned, we saw it was Luca Barnes. His narrow shoulders were hunched and his hands were stuffed tightly in his pockets.

"What are you doing here?" I said, fiercely.

"Look, I come in peace. Can I play?" he asked.

I looked at Daniel and Arj. I knew Luca wasn't really a bad person, but he had been mean to Arj.

"I'm sorry about yesterday. I really am. I was just messing." he said, looking at each of us in turn. I looked at Arj again. He squinted into the sun.

"Do you mind if he plays?" I asked.

Arj looked at his feet and shrugged.

"It's fine, I guess."

"Okay," I said turning back to face Luca. "But any tricks and I'll set Smoke on you." I looked to my side to see the dog curled in a ball, busily licking herself clean.

"You're the catcher first though," Daniel added.

Luca accepted his role and we all prepare to make our way to various parts of the field. In run-outs, the runners have to reach the home base without being touched by the catcher. If you get caught, you're out and you have to join the catching team. When we play at school, Arj is normally the first to get caught but I've been trying to teach him how to improve.

"Listen, Arj. Just remember what I told you." I said, just before the game started. "Stay calm and relaxed. You can't run fast when you tense up."

Arj nodded and headed off in quiet contemplation. His face was stiff and determined. I tied smoke up against the stump so he wouldn't give my position away and we all hid in separate corners of the field.

"GO!" Luca shouted.

I crept slowly around the edge of the designated playing area, staying low and quiet. The start of the game is always tense as everyone waits for someone else to make the first move. A fresh breeze brushed through the tall grass and wildflowers rocked gently back and forth. I peered to my left and could see Arj on all fours, shuffling through the undergrowth. I looked to my right, but I couldn't see Daniel. Luca was still at the home base, looking carefully for any sign of movement.

He didn't have to wait long.

Suddenly, the bushes on the far side of the field were brushed aside and Daniel leapt out into the open and burst into a run. He sprinted straight forward at full speed. At first, Luca seemed not to notice. However, he soon realised what was happening and sprung into action by scuttling across to block Daniel's path. If Luca could touch him, Daniel would lose and have to join Luca's side.

The gap between them decreased massively until they were almost face-to-face with Daniel still running as fast as he could. To my right, I saw Arj moving up more quickly. He wasn't the fastest, but he was smart. He moved forward through the grass, looking to take advantage while Luca was distracted.

I looked back towards the action. Daniel was just a few metres away from Luca. My brother made his move. He dropped his shoulder, feinted one way, then quickly shifted his weight and shot to the other side. Luca's eyes followed the feint, but his feet didn't move. He stood his ground as Daniel made a heroic leap…

Daniel flung himself to the right as Luca's hand stretched out to grab him. Daniel could see the home base. If he could just avoid Luca's grasp he'd win the game. He dug deep and made one last effort to reach the tree, but Luca wasn't finished yet. He planted his feet in the dirt, bent low and then jumped. Luca launched himself towards Daniel and… grabbed him by the shoulder.

Daniel stumbled to a halt and bent double to catch his breath.

"Got ya!" Luca said, proudly. "Good effort, though."

"Thanks," Daniel replied, begrudgingly.

Luca and Daniel barely had time to think before Arj made his move. From the tall grass to my left, Arj emerged. He stood bolt upright and made a break for the tree stump. His arms swung wildly by his side as his little legs carried him as fast as they could.

Luca instantly spotted the danger and raced into action. Daniel, on the other hand, was slower to defend the home base. Luca scrambled across to take up a defensive position. Daniel ambled behind as Arj ran flat-out towards his target. The window of opportunity was closing quickly, but he had a good head start.

Arj's timing was so good that he'd passed Luca and Daniel and had a clear run to the stump. I watched on from my position at the back of the field, willing Arj on every step of the way. He was several metres in front of the catchers and was running faster than I'd ever seen him run before. However, his body language soon changed. He turned his head and frantically looked over his shoulder. It looked like Luca was shouting something, trying to put him off. All of a sudden, I could sense Arj tense up. His shoulders stiffened and his arms became more rigid.

"Relax!" I shouted, but he couldn't hear me. None of them could.

Arj's speed dropped off. His tense body was inefficient and he slowed down dramatically. The more effort he exerted, the slower he went. Soon Luca, and even Daniel, was right behind him. They reached out and grabbed him by the shoulder.

Arj had been caught. Now, it was me against all three catchers. I was massively outnumbered but they were all out of breath. I had to move quickly. I crept through the bushes and skirted the edge of the field, all the time keeping my eyes on Arj, Daniel and Luca.

Eventually, I came to a point where I couldn't hide any longer. The bushes on either side of me faded away. The field opened into a level clearing and Dead Man's Woods prevented me from moving any further to the side. I had two options, either make a break for it and try to outrun all three defenders or move even closer to the woods. I knew I could beat Arj for speed, maybe even Daniel, but Luca would be trickier.

I looked to my right and saw the trees looming over me. The others would never expect me to be so close to Dead Man's Woods. I decided to take the risk. They were just old trees, they couldn't hurt me. I inched closer and the atmosphere around me changed. The wind died down and the sounds of summer disappeared. I could no longer hear birds singing or children playing in the distance. All around me was completely silent.

CHAPTER EIGHT

SUDDENLY, I FELT a chill crawl over my skin. I shivered. I decided I no longer wanted to be near Dead Man's Woods. I stood up and ran. However, Luca and the others had moved closer while I was distracted. They'd figured out my plan and were just a few metres away.

I had to move quickly. If I didn't, they'd catch me easily. I ran to the right and burst past Arj. He made a token effort to catch me but quickly gave up. I knew Luca and Daniel wouldn't be so easy. I ran forward, dropping my shoulder to the left, then to the right. I curved my run to make it harder to predict. They took up a defensive formation and fanned out to cover the most ground. They were smart. We'd played before and they knew my tactics. I'd have to come up with something new.

I ran straight towards Daniel, dropped my shoulder to the right and then skipped to the left. He fell for the feint but recovered quickly. He shifted his weight and leapt through the air. His outstretched arm almost reached me but I managed to arch my back just in time to dodge. I'd avoided Daniel's first effort, but Luca had come across to cover.

I had to abandon the attempt. I circled back the way I'd come to plan a new attack. I put some distance between us and stopped to gather my breath. The woods loomed over me to the right and the boys were between me and the stump. I sucked at the warm air and filled my lungs. I had to try again. I couldn't let Luca or, even worse, my brother win.

I started jogging towards them. They reacted quickly and got into position. Their expressions were serious, they meant business. I picked up my speed and bent my run until I was directly between Luca and Daniel. Then, I went for it. I put my head down and ran as fast as I could between both of them. They figured out my plan and quickly ran to cover the gap.

I moved as rapidly as I could, but the space was closing by the second. A few more steps and they would be on me, one from either side. I could see Luca's smirking face bearing down on me. I couldn't let him win. I kept running but then, at the last second, I stopped.

They weren't expecting it. I skidded to a halt and they, with their eyes still fixed on me, clattered into each other. A cloud of dust mushroomed up from the ground as they fell hard and moaned in agony. Taking no time to savour the sight of their crumpled bodies, I skipped past and made it to the stump as the winner. I raised my arms in the air and jumped high in celebration.

"I AM THE CHAMPION. NO TIME FOR LOSERS!" I sang, loudly.

In the distance, I could see Arj smiling and laughing. Behind him, Dead Man's Woods stood, enormous and dark. I looked again at Luca and Daniel. They were arguing, each one blaming the other for their failure. I laughed some more and looked back to Arj. Except, he wasn't there.

I looked quickly across the field, but he wasn't there either. He was nowhere to be seen. Arj had disappeared and there was only one place he could've gone.

CHAPTER NINE

I RAN TOWARDS where Arj last stood. The patch of dirt was empty and there was nowhere he could've been hiding. I span around and looked desperately for any signs of him.

"What's wrong, Cass?" Daniel asked, having seen my confusion.

"Where's the other one?" Luca added, flatly.

I looked them in the eyes and then turned to face Dead Man's Woods.

"He…?" Daniel started to understand. "In there?"

I nodded slowly.

"He can't have gone in there." Luca stuttered. "There are things in there …*dead things.*"

"Oh come on," I said, rolling my eyes. "You don't really believe that, do you?"

"Wait," Daniel said, before Luca could answer. "Phone him. You have his number, right?"

Of course. How could I have been so stupid? I fumbled in my pocket, pulled out my phone and called Arj.

"Nothing," I said, taking the handset away from my ear to look at the screen. "Just dial tone."

"I thought that might happen," Daniel said. "No signal around here."

"We have to go in. We have to find him." I said, more to myself than to the others.

A cold wind brushed over us. The trees heaved from side to side and the leaves rustled noisily. We were stood on the edge of the woods, but the interior still seemed a million miles away.

"Uh, I think my lunch is ready," Luca said, suddenly. "I have to go!"

"What a wimp," Daniel said, watching Luca turn and flee across the field and towards the houses. The sun glimmered off his watch as he paced back through the grass.

I inched forward, Daniel at my side, and approached the woods. A small gap between two large oak trees gave us a way in.

"This way," I whispered.

I stepped forward and entered Dead Man's Woods and the outside world vanished. The temperature dropped and everything went quiet. The ground was littered with dead leaves and fallen branches that cracked and echoed with every step. I heard Daniel breathing heavily behind me as we slowly made our way deeper into the woods.

There was no sign of Arj. I wanted to call his name, but the thought of breaking the silence seemed somehow wrong, like we were in a church or a library. Instead, we edged further into the darkness. Every step we took echoed loudly, the sound bouncing off the fat tree trunks.

"He has to be here somewhere," I uttered.

"Maybe he just went home?" Daniel replied.

"I'd have seen him, and besides, he's always… wait. What was that?"

Daniel heard it too. There was something in the bushes. The leaves were rustling and dirt was being kicked up. It was getting closer.

Daniel grabbed my arm and braced himself. My eyes still hadn't fully adjusted to the dark so I squinted through the trees for a better look. I couldn't see anything.

Suddenly, I thought back to last night and the thing I'd seen. Why did I come into Dead Man's Woods? How could I be so stupid? The thing with the long arms and boney, jangly legs could be right in front of us and I wouldn't know until it was too late.

There was another sound.

Daniel's hand gripped my arm tightly and I could hear his quick, shallow breath rattle in his chest. A snap of a twig to the right. Something else was there. Something was walking through the woods. I took a step backwards.

We were surrounded.

CHAPTER TEN

LEAVES RUSTLED AND sticks snapped on either side of us. Daniel and I inched closer together. Back-to-back, we span around. It was too dark to see what was coming. Then, suddenly, something sprung from the bushes.

A gigantic black beast leapt towards us and… wagged its tail. It was Smoke. I grabbed her by the collar and turned to face the other noise. Smoke licked excitedly at my wrist. I looked up. The noise was getting louder.

Eventually, a figure stumbled out of the darkness.

"Oh, you found her," Arj said, pointing at the dog.

"Arj!" Daniel and I shouted. "What are you doing in here? What happened?"

Arj looked shocked. His wide-eyes span around the woodland as if he had only just realised where he was.

"I, uh… I saw Smoke. She got off her lead so I chased after her," he said, apologetically. "I knew you'd get in trouble if we lost her."

"You know this is Dead Man's Woods, right?" Daniel asked.

"Yeah, well, no," Arj replied, stepping closer to us and the dog. "I kinda forgot. I just saw Smoke and went."

"You're a strange kid," Daniel said, shaking his head and laughing to himself.

"Yeah," I added, with a smile. "But thanks."

Arj smiled back. Bits of twig were stuck in his hair.

"I tell you what, though," Daniel said, taking some time to inspect a nearby tree. "This place is actually pretty cool."

I didn't answer. I turned on the spot and inspected my surroundings. Something didn't feel right.

"Look at this one," he continued, pointing to a giant oak. "It's huge!"

Arj took a step towards Daniel and looked up towards the top of the tree.

"I think we should get back to the field," I said.

"That one's even bigger," Arj said, pointing to a pine further in the woods. Daniel ran over to it and peered skywards. Dust and leaves fell in his face. He wiped his eyes and laughed.

"Guys, let's head back," I said, but it was no use. Daniel had seen an even taller tree. They both ran to it and inspected the thickness of its trunk. I had no choice but to follow. I let go of Smoke's collar and she ran between the three of us. She was almost as excited as Daniel.

The trees were huge. It was hard to appreciate their size from outside but, from up close, we could see how wide and tall they really were. The canopy blocked out almost all the daylight and the floor was dark and barren. The dry mud slid beneath my feet as I walked. The smell of damp pine filled my nostrils.

Daniel and Arj ran from tree to tree, occasionally stopping to try and fit their arms around the massive trunks. I kept walking to keep up but I could tell we were edging deeper and deeper into the woods. Eventually, all traces of the outside world had disappeared. I turned on the spot. I couldn't remember the way we'd come. I called to the others but they didn't hear. My heart started beating harder in my chest. Something wasn't right. We had to get out.

I started to jog towards Daniel and Arj, their voices faint as they disappeared and reappeared from behind trees. As I saw them up ahead, something else caught my attention. Something inhuman. I froze. I could see Arj and Daniel playing with Smoke. We were all here so who, or what, did I just see?

Slowly, I turned. Shivers ran up my arms and legs.

I looked backwards and screamed.

CHAPTER ELEVEN

THERE WAS SOMETHING in the trees. I saw it move. Something was watching us. Stalking us. A shadow darted out from behind the trunks and disappeared again a second later. I span around. Another shadow, gone in an instant. My breath abandoned me as I turned to run.

Daniel and Arj heard my scream and came closer. I stumbled forward, looking back frantically at the shadow in the trees.

"RUN!" I shouted, the words sticking in my throat.

They were confused but they followed me. I sprinted away from the shadows. I didn't know where I was going but I didn't care, as long as it was away from the thing in the woods. Smoke ran effortlessly alongside me, stopping occasionally to let me catch up. It was a game to her, but not to me. I ran at full speed, jumping logs and sliding past trees.

My lungs started to burn and my thighs were aching before I slowed down to look around. Daniel and Arj were gone. I turned in a circle, frantically looking for them or a way out of the woods. Everywhere I looked there were trees. The meagre light from the sky above had all but disappeared and there was a chill in the air as a gust of wind whipped around my ankles. I could hear myself breathing heavily as I peered into the darkness.

Smoke had stopped too and was sniffing the ground. Her nose still twitched, but her tail had stopped wagging. She whimpered and ran. I called her name but it was too late.

I was all alone. There was no sound and I could barely see. The tall trees blocked out the sky and every way I turned looked the same.

I could feel tears gathering in my eyes as I looked desperately around for any sign of a way out. I called loudly for Arj or Daniel or Smoke, but no-one came. Then, slowly, I became aware of something watching me.

I could sense it standing in the darkness between the trees. All I could see were greys and blacks but I could sense a shift in the light. Something stood silently, just out of reach. I tried to focus my eyes to make out what it was. As I squinted, the figure emerged.

A silhouette stood menacingly against the blackness, its boney limbs jutting out at awkward angles. It was tall and thin. I gasped and stepped back again.

"Who's there?" I called, my voice trembling.

CHAPTER TWELVE

"CASSIE!" DANIEL CALLED.

I looked behind to see him and Arj tramping their way through the bracken. Smoke was at their side.

"Wait!" I yelled. "Don't come closer!"

I whirled around again to the silhouette but it was gone. The deep, impenetrable blackness of where it was standing had turned light grey and I could see through to the trees behind. A dead leaf fell from the sky and rocked gently to the floor.

"Cassie! Come on!" Arj said. "Let's get out of here."

He was right. We had to go. I walked slowly backwards, not wanting to take my eyes off where it had been, then I turned and ran.

I followed Arj and Daniel through the woods. Eventually, the darkness was perforated by rays of light as the canopy opened up and we reached the edge of the woods. I could see the daylight beyond.

"That was crazy!" Daniel said as we stumbled into the field again. Sunlight flooded back over my skin.

"What happened?" Arj asked, looking concerned.

"I saw it," I said, struggling to catch my breath. "The thing from last night. I saw it."

Daniel laughed.

"I'm not joking!" I yelled. "It was right in front of me."

"What thing? What did it look like?" Arj asked, his eyes wide.

"She thinks there's a monster in the woods," Daniel scoffed, turning to Arj. "Just ignore her."

"Not a monster!" I replied. I could feel my face starting to burn. "Well, maybe. I don't know what it was."

"I believe you, Cassie," Arj said, softly.

"Then you're both crazy!"

"I know what I saw, Daniel," I said.

"Do you? Do you really?" he replied, his eyebrows raised. "It was so dark in there that we could hardly see our hands in front of our faces, but you saw this *thing* clearly, did you?"

I paused. I was still breathing heavily. The sun was still bright and strong. The heat burned onto the back of my neck. Slowly, warmth returned to the rest of my body.

"Well, not clearly but…"

"And you don't think it's possible that you were wrong?" Daniel ranted. "That it was something else. A tree branch. A deer. Someone trying to scare you?"

"Why would someone want to scare us?" Arj asked, looking frightened again.

I went to speak but stopped myself. Maybe Daniel was right. Maybe I was mistaken. Then, suddenly, I remembered something and everything became clear.

I knew exactly what was happening.

CHAPTER THIRTEEN

IT WAS LUCA!

I should've known as soon as I saw those gangly arms and legs. He was playing another trick on me. Trying to scare me as payback for pushing him. I should never have trusted him. As we walked back towards the houses, I saw him. He was standing over the dead deer, poking it with a stick.

"You think you're funny?" I said, walking straight up to him. The smell of rotten meat drifted up to greet us.

"Huh? Oh, you found Arj. That's good." he said, looking up from the deer.

"I thought you had to get lunch? Or was that another lie?" I said, angrily. I could feel myself losing control.

"I had lunch already." he said, looking to Daniel and Arj. "You've been gone ages."

"So, I suppose you're gonna deny it?" I asked, hands on hip.

"Deny what, Cassie? Why are you so angry?"

"Trying to scare me in the woods." I blurted. "Standing in the darkness, watching us like a weirdo."

"I …don't know what you're talking about. I've been playing here by myself." he said, holding up the stick he'd been poking the deer with. A maggot clung bravely onto the tip. I couldn't believe he was going to deny the whole thing. I felt my cheeks flushing again as my frustration grew.

"Come on, Cass," Daniel said, sensing my mood. "Let's go home."

I knew Daniel was right. I'd get in trouble if I lost my temper again. I turned and brushed past the boys. From behind, I heard Luca's voice call out.

"Did you get scared in Dead Man's Woods?" he said, laughing loudly.

I didn't stop. If I turned around, I knew I'd do something I'd regret. I kept walking but heard Daniel say something that made Luca stop laughing. I smiled to myself as I imagined what it was.

We said goodbye to Arj and made our way home. Mum was waiting in the kitchen with cheese and ham sandwiches. She'd cut them into triangles how I like them.

"There you are! My brave adventurers!" hhe said, pulling us in for a hug.

"MUM!" we moaned in unison.

"Oh, let her have her fun," Dad said from the table. "She's been missing you."

"She nearly broke my back!" Daniel said.

"What have you been getting up to this morning?" Mum said, handing over some freshly squeezed orange juice to go with the food.

"Run-outs," I mumbled, with a mouthful of cheese and ham.

"Ooh, how lovely," Mum said.

"Who won?" Dad added.

"I did!" I said, proudly. Daniel's silence confirmed my victory.

"You've been playing run-outs this whole time?" Mum asked. "You must be exhausted."

"No," Daniel said, looking at me. "We went into the woods for a bit."

Mum and Dad stopped what they were doing and looked him in the eyes. The room fell silent.

"Dead Man's Woods?" Dad asked, eventually.

I nodded. Dad looked worried. He glanced towards Mum and they shared a look.

"What do you want to be going into a place like that for?" Mum asked, forcing herself to sound casual. She ran a hand through her hair and leaned against the counter.

"Smoke ran in there. We had to get her." I said, feeling strangely like I had to defend myself. I took another bite of my sandwich. The ham-to-cheese ratio was just right.

"Smoke?" Mum repeated. The dog heard her name and padded his way across the kitchen. Her stumpy tail wagged back and forth.

"Bad dog!" Dad said, sternly. Smoke whimpered and lowered her head. "You do not go running off."

"It wasn't her fault!" I pleaded. "Her lead came loose."

I looked at Daniel. I could tell he was thinking the same as me. Why were our parents so mad at Smoke? Dad loved her almost as much as he loved me and

Daniel. He never told her off if he didn't have to. Yet, he just yelled at her for running into Dead Man's Woods.

The woods! That's it. Mum and Dad both acted strange last time we mentioned Dead Man's Woods. What's wrong? Why don't they want us going to the woods? Why are they so scared?

I wish I'd never found out.

CHAPTER FOURTEEN

THAT EVENING, MY room was hot and muggy again as I tried to sleep. I flipped my pillow and rolled from side to side, but I couldn't get comfortable. I stood up and shuffled over to the window. I forced myself to look to the woods.

I couldn't see anything. It was too dark and the shadows were unmoving. I pushed the window open and sat back down on the edge of my bed. I could hear the faint sound of Daniel's laptop blaring music from his room. I thought back to the conversation with Luca. He wasn't usually such a good liar. Normally, his stupid grin would give him away, but he kept a straight face the whole time.

He was almost believable, but it had to be him. There was no other explanation. A million thoughts raced through my mind as the streetlight outside flickered and shut off. My room was now almost completely black. The street was quiet. All our neighbours had gone to bed.

I laid back down on top of the covers, wishing for a breeze to make its way through the window. My bed creaked slightly as I shifted position. I turned the pillow again and rested my face against the cool fabric as I heard a noise from the far side of the room.

I opened my eyes. My wardrobe door was open. I was sure I'd closed it when I got changed. *Hadn't I?* I swung my legs to the ground and moved slowly across the room with only the dim moonlight to guide me. The long shadows of books and clothes stretched across the carpet. I moved slowly, carefully placing my feet to avoid treading on the things I'd discarded in the day.

I swung the door back and forth on its hinges and then pushed it shut. It wasn't broken. The latch was working perfectly and the door stayed in place. I turned to walk back to my bed, but I saw something out the corner of my eye.

Slowly, I turned my head to the right. There, on the far side of my room, was a shadow. I froze. The dark mass raised its head and stared right at me. I tried to scream but no sound came out. It raised its long, boney arms from its sides and took a step forwards.

CHAPTER FIFTEEN

I COULD FEEL my knees shaking and my throat
tightening. My feet felt as heavy as bricks as I forced
them back towards my bed. I stepped clumsily,
tripping and stumbling on a pair of shoes and a book
laying on the floor.

The thing in the corner of the room opened its
mouth and let out an unnatural growl. It bent slightly
and sprung forward. I screamed and jumped to the
side. I smashed into my fan and sent it flying.
Scrambling on all fours, I made my way to the door
as the thing gathered itself for another attack. Its
boney elbows stuck out at right-angles to the side.

It jumped towards me and smashed into the wall
as I managed to slip through the door just in time. I
barged into Daniel's room but he wasn't there. A
video was playing on his laptop but his bed was
empty. I turned round to see the thing enter the room.
Its arms and legs scraped against the door frame as it
saw me in the corner.

It burst forward and lunged again, but I was too
quick. I leapt to the side and rolled over the bed. The

thing fell hard into the far wall. I ran from the room and down the stairs. I braced myself against the doorframe and flew around into the kitchen. Daniel was stood, staring into the fridge.

"Daniel!" I yelled. "RUN!"

He didn't answer.

He continued staring straight ahead with his back to me. I ran up to him, put my hand on his pointy shoulder and spun him around. His back clicked and his neck spasmed.

It wasn't him.

It looked like him, but his features had changed. His nose was wonky and his eyes were completely black. His arms were long and stuck out at awkward angles. He was one of them…

I screamed and ran from the room as Daniel lurched towards me, his dead eyes following me as I went. I had to go. I had to get help. I opened the door to the living room and called for Mum and Dad.

They didn't answer either.

They were stood in front of the TV, their long, spindly limbs almost filling the room. Dad turned to me and growled. My mouth dropped open in shock as the other zombies entered the room. Delirious and confused, I stumbled back against the wall as all four of them slowly moved towards me.

CHAPTER SIXTEEN

I WAS TRAPPED. I tried to scream, but nothing came out. My mouth was open but everything was silent until I heard a voice calling me.

"Cassie!"

I looked around but I couldn't see anyone other than the four monstrous zombies closing in on me. I could smell their sweat as they raised their arms and moved closer. Their stale breath oozed out of their strange mouths.

"Cassie!"

Again, I searched for the source of the voice. I turned and twisted, desperately looking for help. Then, suddenly, my shoulders spasmed and my entire body jolted back and forth.

"Cassie. Wake up."

I opened my eyes. Daniel was standing over me. He was fully dressed and ready to go out.

"It's 11 am," he said, removing his hands from my shoulders. "Arj is downstairs, he wants to hang out." I looked around the room. Sweat was dripping from my forehead. Daniel's face was… normal. His arms and legs were the right size and his eyes were the usual shade of brown.

It was all a dream.

I couldn't believe it. It had all seemed so real. I could still smell their putrid flesh and rotten teeth. My heart was still racing as Daniel left the room. I got washed and dressed and met him and Arj downstairs.

It was another bright and beautiful day. The sun streamed in through the windows and cast a mellow haze throughout the kitchen. I put my nightmare to the back of my mind and left the house. A lone wisp of cloud drifted across the electric blue sky.

"Let's go to Dead Man's Woods!" Daniel said. "There were so many cool places to explore."

I looked at Arj. He seemed to be thinking the same as me.

"I'm not sure that's a good idea," I mumbled.

"Oh, come on!" Daniel replied. "Don't be such a wimp! We know it was just Luca trying to scare us, so we'll be ready for it this time, won't we?"

He had a point. It had to be Luca, and he wouldn't get away with it again.

"Okay, let's do it," I said. Arj looked at me with his eyebrows raised.

"Awesome!" Daniel squealed. "Plus," he added, looking at Arj. "You'll always have Smoke to protect you."

Arj looked down at Smoke. The dog's tongue was hanging out the side of her mouth and her head was cocked to the side.

"Great," Arj said, rolling his eyes.

As we passed through the alleyway and crossed the field, the woods loomed as large as ever. A stiff wind greeted us as we approached the trees. I shivered but forced myself to continue. Daniel and Smoke ran ahead. Arj and I followed slowly behind.

Inside the entrance to the woods, the noise from outside faded away. It was just us and the trees. Daniel's voice punctured the silence as he ran among the thick trunks. Arj picked up a stick and threw it for Smoke.

"At least she's having a good time," I thought, watching the dog happily drag a broken branch around the base of an old sycamore tree. We walked all throughout the wood, taking in the different plant life before, suddenly, I heard Daniel call out.

"CASSIE!" he yelled from behind some shrubs. "ARJ!"

We both ran to see what was wrong. When we reached him, he looked different. He was shorter than normal. I looked at his feet and realised why. Daniel had sunk to his ankles in mud. Thick, wet, gloopy mud.

He looked up at me and laughed.

"Look at this stuff," he said, trying to wiggle his right leg free. "I'm completely stuck!"

"Well, it was fun knowing you!" I said, turning to leave. "Bye forever!"

"Har-har," he said, sarcastically. "Get a stick or something and help me out."

Arj was already thinking ahead and grabbed a branch from Smoke's mouth. The dog sat back excitedly wagging her tail.

"Here, take this," Arj said, carefully not treading in the sticky mud.

"Aww, can't we just leave him in there a little longer?" I pleaded. "A few months maybe."

"I will shove your face in this mud when I get out, Cass!"

"Correction. *If* you get out," I replied, smiling.

He grasped the end of Arj's stick and we both pulled on it until he started to inch forward. Eventually, Daniel managed to work enough wiggle room to free himself from the mud. He clambered forward on all fours and collapsed onto the firm forest floor next to us.

"That was crazy!" Daniel said, rolling onto his back and splaying his arms out to the side.

"Mum's going to kill you," I replied, looking at the state of his mud-soaked shoes.

Arj chucked the big stick we'd used further into the muddy patch. It looped high up into the sky and plopped straight into the middle of the clearing. Then, we watched on as the entire length of the stick slowly sunk down into the deep, deep mud. The surface bubbled for a second before returning to how it was before. It was as if the stick had never existed.

"That stick was bigger than you, Daniel," Arj said, his mouth agape.

"Are you saying, if I'd walked a bit further in, that could've been me sinking all the way in there?"

Arj nodded.

"Sick!" Daniel said, with a grin.

"Maybe we should try it out. See if it works," I said, pretending to shove Daniel into the mud.

"How about this big rock instead?" Arj offered.

"Hmm, I suppose that could work," I replied, walking over to help lift the heavy stone by Arj's feet.

We heaved it over to the edge of the mud and the three of us launched it high into the air. It landed with a squelch and instantly started sinking. In a matter of seconds, the whole thing had disappeared beneath the surface.

"That's insane!" I said in disbelief as the final bubble popped on the surface where the stone had landed seconds before.

"Do you think there are other patches like this around here?" Arj asked.

"I hope so!" Daniel replied.

"I'm serious, we could stumble into them and get trapped."

"Arj is right," I said. "We should probably leave."

"Fine!" Daniel sighed. "You guys are such wimps."

As we turned to go, there was a rustling sound from behind us that stopped me in my tracks.

"Who's there?" Daniel asked, but there was no response. Arj took a step closer to me as we heard the noise again.

"Luca, is that you?" I asked loudly. "It's not funny anymore."

"Yeah, pack it in Luca," Daniel added. "We're not scared of you."

The noise didn't stop. In fact, it got louder. Soon, the rustling was just a few metres away, but it was so dark in the woods that we couldn't see who or what was making it. Suddenly, Arj started rummaging in his pocket and, a second later, produced a bright white light from his phone.

"Good thinking!" I said, as he pointed it at the source of the noise.

There was nothing there.

A tree behind us groaned. Arj swung the light around and our eyes followed it. We looked past the large trunk and saw something dash out of sight. Something big. Arj spun the light in every direction but he couldn't find it.

"Cassie…" he said. "I think we should go now."

"I think you're right," I replied, my eyes still scouring the darkness for any movement.

"This way!" Daniel said, pulling his own phone out of his pocket and turning on the torch. I did the same and followed him. Our three beams of light whirled around us, frantically trying to illuminate as much of the woods as possible.

Our initial walk quickly became a jog as the blackness of Dead Man's Woods closed in around us. As we passed a chunky oak tree, the sound returned on our left. In unison, we all lit it up but there was nothing there. We stopped jogging and waited. We'd all heard it. The sound of someone or something right next to us was unmistakable. We'd stopped in the middle of a small clearing and, for a moment, it was silent.

Then, a large branch crashed to the floor beside us. The noise ricocheted around the woods. We paused for a second and looked upwards at the canopy before another branch thudded onto the ground just behind us. Then another, and another.

We were under attack.

CHAPTER SEVENTEEN

"RUN!" I SHOUTED.

We darted through the woods at top speed as tree branches rained down all around us. As I skipped over a fallen log, I heard Arj yell in pain. I skidded to a stop and turned back. He'd tripped and was laying in the dirt as sticks and logs clattered him from all angles.

I ran back and grabbed him by the shoulders. A branch zoomed past my face and skipped across the ground. We stood up and ran as more branches fell. Daniel hadn't realised we'd stopped and was far ahead. I could just see the light from his phone glinting between trees in the distance. I followed it with Arj right behind me. We made our way through the woods, ducking and weaving as we went to avoid the bits of trees flying through the air.

Eventually, light from outside started to spear its way through the gaps in the trees. The spaces between trunks grew wider and the bombardment slowed. Arj and I burst through a smattering of small, leafy branches and were instantly drenched in magnificent sunlight. Daniel was waiting in the field, wielding a thick log as a bat.

"I don't think you'll need that!" I said, struggling to catch my breath. "No-one's following us."

"Are you okay?" Daniel asked, looking at Arj's many cuts and bruises.

"Yeah," he replied, twisting his arm and stretching his neck to get a better look at a gash on the far side.

"You're tougher than you look, Arj," Daniel added, patting him on the back.

"Thanks, I guess."

"What the heck was that?" I said, cutting across them both. My breaths were shallow and quick and my hands were shaking. "Luca has gone crazy."

"He could've really hurt us," Daniel said. "He's gone too far this time."

"Maybe it wasn't Luca," Arj added, quietly.

"Of course it was. Who else could it have been? Luca's the only one mad enough."

"But the logs were coming from different angles," Arj reasoned.

"So, he had help." Daniel shot back. "I assume he's got friends?" He added, looking in my direction. I shrugged. I genuinely didn't know.

"What do you think, Cass?" Arj asked.

"I agree with Daniel. It has to be him."

Arj said nothing. He bent down and rubbed a graze on his leg. A blue and yellow bruise was already forming.

"Thank you!" Daniel squealed, "finally someone seeing sense!"

"He could've really hurt you Arj. That's not cool."

"He really didn't want us to be in there," Daniel said.

"But, why?" I asked. "Why is Luca trying to scare us away from Dead Man's Woods?"

CHAPTER EIGHTEEN

THE NEXT MORNING, I woke up early to visit Arj. He'd suffered a lot of cuts and bruises from the attack in Dead Man's Woods, so I wanted to make sure he was okay.

"Where are you off to?" Mum asked as I headed out the door.

"Just going to hang out with Arj," I answered. "Play video games."

I'd decided not to tell my parents about what happened the day before. They'd warned us about Dead Man's Woods and this whole thing would just make them more uptight about it.

"Okay, have fun sweetie!" Mum called, as I was halfway down the path. I waved as I skipped through the gate. Arj's house was just a couple of streets away and his family were always welcoming to me.

I took a shortcut through an alleyway, reached his house and knocked on the door. His dad let me in and pointed me upstairs. I kicked off my shoes and headed on up. The thick carpet was plush and soft beneath my feet.

"How are you feeling?" I asked as Arj let me in. His room was small but very neat. Everything was tidy and in the right place. Why couldn't Daniel keep his room like this?

"I'm fine, honestly," he replied. "Physically, at least."

"What do you mean?"

"I mean, cuts and bruises heal," he said, rotating his forearm and inspecting the grazes along the length of it.

"But?"

"But we've got a bigger problem," he added, sitting lightly down on his perfectly made bed. On the bedside table was a framed photo of me, him and Daniel at my birthday party a few weeks ago.

"You mean Luca?" I asked. He stared up at me.

"Maybe," he said, finally. "…but maybe it wasn't him, Cass."

"Oh god, not this again," I sighed. "There are no zombies in Dead Man's Woods!"

"Then what did you see?" he said, animatedly. "From your window. What was that?"

"I don't know," I confessed. "I was tired. Maybe I was dreaming again."

"Come on, Cassie. You know you weren't dreaming."

"This is ridiculous!" I said, desperately. "I will prove it. I will get to the bottom of it and show you how stupid you're being."

Arj didn't speak. Instead, I got to my feet and left. I could feel my frustration rising again and I didn't want to fall out with Arj. I padded down the stairs and slipped into my shoes.

"Oh, that was short and sweet," Arj's dad said. "I was just going to bring you some snacks."

I forced a smile and thanked him for the thought.

"See you again soon, Cassie!" he said, waving goodbye as I walked down the drive. On the way home, I saw a tall, skinny figure at the end of the alleyway.

Luca Barnes.

I ran to catch him up.

"What's your problem?" I yelled, as I got close.

He slowly turned to look at me.

"I told you," he snarled. A sickening smile spread across his thin lips. "I told you to stay away from Dead Man's Woods."

CHAPTER NINETEEN

"I KNOW IT was you!" I growled.

"I warned you," he replied, calmly. His small, beady eyes got even narrower.

"Why did you do it? Arj is really scratched up."

"Me?" he said, taken aback. "I didn't do anything."

His expression and body language changed. He took a step back, raised his eyebrows and screwed up his face.

"Don't lie to me, Luca," I said. "I know it was you throwing those logs."

"I heard what happened, Cassie, but it wasn't me."

"I can't believe you're denying it," I shot back. "Who else could it have been? No-one else knew we were going there."

"It's the …*things,*" he said, more seriously. "The zombie things. I tried to warn you about them."

His thin lips straightened and his pale face turned even whiter.

"Don't start with that nonsense!" I shouted.

Suddenly, there was a voice from behind us.

"What's going on?" Daniel asked, seeing us arguing.

"Nothing," Luca said. "I'm going now, anyway."

Daniel stood next to me as Luca barged past and made his way up the alleyway.

"What was all that about?" he asked when Luca was out of earshot.

"He's denying it all," I said, rubbing my face with my hands. "Can you believe that?"

Daniel didn't speak, but his face told me everything.

"Don't tell me, you're believing in zombies too, now?" I asked. "Has everybody gone crazy?"

"No," he said, firmly. "It's just that, maybe we were a bit too hasty yesterday. Maybe we should think about it more before we accuse him again."

"Since when were you the beacon of reason and second chances?" I quipped.

Daniel laughed. We left the alley and took a seat on a nearby bench. The road was quiet. A neighbour washed his car in a driveway in the distance. I felt the hot sun on the back of my neck as I leaned forward on my elbows.

"Right," Daniel said. "Let's look at the facts."

"Have you been watching those detective shows again?"

"Shut up. Let's take this seriously."

"Okay," I said, still smiling. "First of all, he's always talking about Dead Man's Woods and the things that live there. He really wants us to think he believes all those stories about zombies in the shadows…"

"I think Arj believes them, and he's really smart."

"Let's stick to Luca, okay?" I said. "On top of believing in children's stories, he's always playing pranks on people. He jumped out the bush at us, remember?"

"Yeah, and you scared him so badly he'd never do it again!" Daniel laughed.

"Well, clearly I didn't scare him that much because now he's taking it to another level."

"Is that all you have?" Daniel questioned. "That he's mean and he's crazy?"

"No," I replied, trying hard to think. "There's more. I've got it!"

"What?"

"That day, when he jumped out on us. He had a saw! Remember? He must have used it to cut down all the branches he chucked at us and Arj. It has to be him!"

Daniel's expression changed. He couldn't deny it any longer.

"You're right," he said, finally. "It really is him."

"I told you so!" I squealed.

"What are we gonna do about it?" Daniel added. "We can't let him get away with it."

"Don't worry. I've got a plan," I said, brushing the hair out my eyes. "It's time we gave Luca Barnes a taste of his own medicine."

CHAPTER TWENTY

WE LEFT THE bench and headed home. The workers were busy in the corner of the garage. Men wearing reflective jackets and hard-hats milled around as sparks flew and dust floated in the still summer air.

"This is perfect," I said, gathering materials behind the builders' backs. I slipped two short bits of drainpipe out of the pile next to our house and handed them to Daniel. Smoke sniffed them eagerly.

"Should we be doing this?" he asked when we got to my room.

"Don't worry, they're off-cuts. They'll just throw them away."

"What's going on, Cass?" he said, as I positioned his arms out to the side and measured them for size. "What's your amazing plan?"

"You'll see!" I said. "Just wait here for one second."

I skipped out the door and quietly entered my parents' bedroom. It was empty. I looked behind the door and saw my Dad's old leather jacket hanging where he'd left it many years ago. I slid it off the hook and made my way back to Daniel.

"What's that for?" he asked, looking at the black jacket in my arms. "Dad's going to kill you."

"They've gone out for lunch with the Millers," I explained. "We'll put it back before they even come home. Now hold out your arms again."

Reluctantly, he did as I asked and I slotted the drainpipes over his outstretched forearms before easing him into the leather jacket. The sleeves were tight around the thick, plastic pipes but I managed to pull them all the way up and into place. Daniel suddenly seemed to understand.

"That's… brilliant!" he said, twirling around in my full-length mirror. "It looks like my arms are massive!"

"We just need one more thing to finish it all off…"

I rummaged around in my drawer and found an old tub of pale foundation that Auntie Jeanie had given me for Christmas last year.

"*You* own make-up?" Daniel asked, grinning.

I took some of the powder on the brush and jabbed it in Daniel's face.

"Ow!" he yelled. "Be gentle!"

"Oh, sorry. Sometimes I don't know my own strength." I smiled.

A few seconds later, I stepped back to admire my work. Daniel turned to look at himself in the mirror one more time.

"Sick!" he said. "I look half dead!"

"That's the idea." I quipped. "We lure Luca to the woods and then you jump out and scare him senseless."

Daniel laughed.

"He's gonna wet himself when he sees me!" he said, holding his elongated arms out and walking around the room like a zombie.

CHAPTER TWENTY-ONE

I SENT A text to Luca and told him I'd found another dead animal to prod. I knew he wouldn't be able to resist such an exciting temptation.

"Where is it then?" Daniel asked as we approached Dead Man's Woods.

"Where's what?" I replied.

"The animal."

I stopped and looked at him. He was being serious.

"It doesn't exist, idiot. I just said it to get Luca here."

"Oh," he sighed. "Yeah, that makes sense."

I laughed and told him to wait behind a nearby tree just inside the woods. It was time to put our plan into action.

"I'll keep Smoke and meet Luca here, then bring him up towards you. When we get to that tree, you jump out. Okay?"

"Roger," Daniel said before waddling off with his unnaturally long arms and bone white face. Coming out of the darkness of the woods, he'd scare anyone.

I sat and waited with my hands on my knees. Smoke sniffed the ground nearby. I looked behind me. I couldn't see Daniel. He was already so well hidden that Luca would never see it coming. Eventually, I saw two figures entering the field. One tall and thin, the other short and squat. As they approached, I realised it was Luca and Arj.

I couldn't believe it. They were the last two people I'd expect to hang out together, and yet there they were, ruining our plan. We only wanted to scare Luca, but now Arj was going to get in the way.

"Hey," I said, looking at Arj. "What are you doing here?"

Luca spoke before Arj could answer.

"I made the mistake of telling him I was coming to meet you," he said. "And he insisted on coming."

Arj took a step forward and stood next to me. He nodded to confirm Luca's story. He looked at me with wide eyes. I wanted to tell him why we didn't invite him, but I couldn't say anything without Luca hearing.

"Okay," I said, trying to think of a way for Daniel not to scare Arj. "On second thoughts, why don't we just play run-outs or something? Dead animals are boring."

"No way!" Luca yelled. " I came all this way…"

"We can see your house from here," Arj said.

"All this way, to see a dead deer!" Luca continued. "And I'm not leaving until I see it. What's the matter? You scared, Cassie?"

"No, it's just that…"

"What about your wimpy brother? Was he too scared to see it, too? Is that why he's not here?"

"That's it," I thought. I'm sorry, Arj, but you're going to have to take one for the team. It's time for Luca to get what he deserves.

"It's just over here," I said. "In Dead Man's Woods. You're not scared, are you?"

"Me? No, never," Luca said, his voice wavering only slightly. "Lead the way."

I looked at Arj. I could tell he didn't want to go back in the woods, but he didn't say anything. The pit of my stomach churned at the thought of him being scared by Daniel. I just hoped he would understand afterwards.

We moved closer to the woods. I could feel Luca's tension rising, but I knew he was too stubborn to turn back. The large, dark trees rose up over our heads and, as we approached, the wind whipped along the side of the field and tugged at our clothing from all angles. Soon, the ground beneath our feet turned from lush, green grass to dry, hard mud. We left daylight behind and entered the darkness of the woods.

"Well?" Luca said, looking frantically from side to side. "Where is it, Cassie? Quickly."

"Just a little bit further," I lied, as we approached the tree Daniel had agreed to hide behind.

Suddenly, out of the blackness, we heard a sound of scuffed footsteps. All three of us spun on our heels and looked in the direction of the noise.

"What was that?" Arj asked.

"I …don't know," I said, honestly. Had Daniel moved? Surely, I'd have seen or heard him before. Then, another noise in the other direction. We span around again.

"Someone's here," Arj whispered.

A branch thudded onto the ground behind us. Then, another to the side. If this was Daniel, he was putting on a great show. Arj, Luca and I span around in all directions as more noises broke out of the silence.

Then, abruptly, a giant figure leapt out of the darkness.

CHAPTER TWENTY-TWO

IT CAUGHT ME off guard and I screamed. Luca roared in terror. Arj ran. The shock took me off my feet and I landed on the ground with a thud. Luca stepped back and trod on my hand, pain seared through my arm but my attention was elsewhere.

Arj was running in the wrong direction. The sounds from the woods confused him and now he wasn't running out towards the field, but straight into the ever-increasing darkness of Dead Man's Woods.

"Arj!" I yelled. "Come back! It's only Daniel!"

He couldn't hear me. He was too far gone and my voice was swallowed up by the vastness of the woods. An echo repeated my words as if the woods themselves were mocking me.

"What's Arj doing here?" Daniel asked, his face white and arms rigid in the drainpipes.

"I knew it was you!" Luca claimed, unconvincingly.

"We need to stop him." I cut across them both. "He's going the wrong way. He's going to get lost."

Daniel slipped his arms out of the pipes and he and Luca followed me as I ran to find Arj. Any light from the outside soon faded away as we passed huge trees on either side. I was faster than Arj, so I knew I could catch him if I hurried. I sprinted as fast as I could into the darkness, calling his name the whole time. I sensed Smoke running by my side, her light feet moving quickly over the dusty earth.

It was no use. Arj was gone. He had disappeared deep into the woods and it was all my fault. It was me who had dressed Daniel up. It was me who decided to proceed with the plan. If Arj got lost in these woods, it's all on me. I stopped to catch my breath. A second later, Daniel and Luca joined me. The light from their phones fell on the dead, barren ground.

"We can't just keep running, Cass," Daniel said, as sweat dripped from his forehead. He was still wearing Dad's leather jacket. The empty sleeves hung way past his hands.

"Let's go back," Luca said. "He'll be fine."

"No," I barked. "We need to find him. He'd do the same for us."

"He must've passed through here," Daniel added. "Let's spread out a bit and walk this way."

I could've hugged him. I would've continued searching by myself, but I really didn't want to. I grabbed my phone from my pocket, turned on the torch, and started walking. Daniel joined on my right and, hesitantly, Luca did the same on my left.

"You were pretty scared back there, Cassie!" Luca whispered as we walked slowly through the trees.

"Shut up," I said.

"I have to admit, Dan," Luca continued. "When you made the noises from behind us, it got a little creepy!"

Daniel paused. He looked at the ground and then back up again. Something was troubling him.

"The noises from behind you?" he asked.

"Yeah," Luca said. "How did you make it sound like you were all around us?"

Daniel furrowed his brow and looked between me and Luca as we waited for his answer.

"I didn't," he said, slowly.

CHAPTER TWENTY-THREE

I LOOKED AT Luca. I knew what he was thinking. If Daniel didn't make those noises who, or *what*, did?

"It must've been an animal," I suggested, looking down at Smoke. I reached down and scratched her behind the ear. Her little tail darted from side-to-side.

"That was no animal, Cassie," Luca said. His face had turned as pale as the make-up on Daniel's.

"Even if it was a *zombie*," I said, making air quotes with my fingers. "That just means we definitely have to find Arj now, doesn't it? He could be in danger."

"No, it doesn't," Luca said, shaking his head. "Not for me. I'm out of here."

"Good luck then," I said, gesturing back the way we'd come. "You'll be able to find your way back alone, right?"

Luca turned in a circle and surveyed the darkness.

"On second thoughts," he said. "I think we should definitely stick together."

"Great idea," I said, rolling my eyes.

"Come on," Daniel said, suddenly. "Let's find Arj and get out of here."

We started walking again. The woods were silent except for the occasional whistle of wind or the crack of a branch. Every few seconds, one of us called Arj's name. The beams of light from our phones whirled around in all directions as we searched for any sign of movement.

Minutes passed and there was still no sign of him. We kept walking and shouting. Occasionally, we'd hear a noise and all spin around to point our lights at the source, but we didn't find anything. The woods looked empty. They looked dead. Then, out the corner of my eye, I saw something.

There was something shiny on the ground. A rare splash of light reflected off it and caught my eye. The crisp leaves bent and broke beneath my feet as I approached to get a closer look.

It was Arj's phone.

"Oh, man!" Luca said.

"That's not good," Daniel added, looking up at me. His face was still powder white and Dad's leather jacket hung down over his hands. It would've looked funny if it wasn't so serious.

"That means he was here recently," I said, trying desperately to be positive.

As I was about to speak again, we heard the sound of scuffed feet and breaking branches nearby. We turned together, shone our torches and I ran towards it. The others followed. I called Arj's name and hoped to see him emerge from the shadows.

We heard the sound again. It was coming from behind the next row of trees. Through the branches, I could just make out a small clearing. We shone our phones but the light couldn't penetrate far enough to see. I brushed a low branch out the way and stepped forward. In the centre of the clearing, a shadow stood alone.

It wasn't Arj.

CHAPTER TWENTY-FOUR

I SHONE MY light on its back. It was tall and skinny, with arms down to its knees. Slowly, its head swivelled and its body creaked. It's dead, black eyes stared straight at me.

I screamed.

The thing bent and turned. Its elbows and knees jutted out at weird angles and it stretched its weird, toothless mouth to gargle a roar in our direction. Suddenly, I felt a hand on my shoulder.

"CASSIE! RUN!" Daniel said, spinning me around on the spot where I'd frozen in place.

I snapped out of my trance in time to see Luca disappearing into the distance. Twigs scratched at my face as I burst forward and smashed through the layer of branches we'd just passed. I looked over my shoulder to make sure Daniel was behind me. He was, but behind him was the zombie. It moved frantically, its massively oversized limbs swooping clumsily through the air as it dragged its bony carcass towards us with all the grace of a punch-drunk elephant.

I saw something dark flash past me and realised it was Smoke. Her whimpers hung in the air as she zoomed away in the same direction as Luca. We tried to follow, but the dog was too fast. She vanished into the woods.

Daniel and I ran as fast as we could. I could hear the zombie smashing through the trees behind us. We skipped between branches, the zombie broke straight through them. Suddenly, something whizzed past my ear and crashed into a trunk in front of us. As it splintered into a thousand pieces, I realised it was coming from the zombie. It was throwing bits of tree at us as it ran.

Luca was telling the truth. He really was innocent.

A smaller branch hit my shoulder, but I managed to keep my balance as we kept running. We had no idea where we were heading. The woods were as dark as ever and we had no time to stop and think. Daniel ran beside me and we both knew our only hope was to stay together.

"This way!" I yelled, veering to the left and hopping over a fallen oak. The old bark crumbled and split as we brushed over it.

I didn't have a plan. For all I knew, I was leading us further and further into the woods, but we had to try something. We turned left, then right, then left again in an effort to lose the zombie. It was no use. It was still right behind us, destroying everything in its path. Then, I saw something.

It was Luca. He was standing perfectly still in the centre of a small clearing. I barged into Daniel and forced him round to the right. We clattered through a wall of thin branches and landed in the clearing beyond.

Luca didn't react.

He stood deadly still with his back to us. The zombie was right behind us so we had to move quickly.

"LUCA!" I yelled as we raced up to him.

"RUN!" Daniel screamed.

Luca didn't move. We soon found out why.

CHAPTER TWENTY-FIVE

AS I LOOKED into Luca's face, he stared right through me. He was looking at something over my shoulder. I followed his eye-line and saw it. Laying just at the edge of the clearing, was a dead deer. Except, this one wasn't alone. A zombie crouched over the rotting carcass with bits of meat and bones hanging loosely from its deformed mouth. Its beady eyes stared right at us as animal blood ran down its chin and up its thin arms.

It was taller than the first one but just as ugly. Its shoulders were hunched and its arms were skinny and elongated. Its bony fingers curled at weird angles and its legs were lumpy and misshapen. Its toothless mouth was covered by a broken and stretched fold of skin and its dark eyes stared at us menacingly from beneath the trees.

At that moment, the first zombie burst into the clearing and skidded to a halt. I could feel Daniel's back push against my own as we stared the two monsters down. The zombies took a slow step forward. We had to get out. It was now or never.

I grabbed Luca by the collar, turned to my left and prepared to run. However, when I looked up, I saw another one. At the side of the clearing, another zombie stood with a hunched back. It stared at us as a long line of spit dribbled from the hole where its mouth should have been. I turned back and faced the other way. There was another on my right. Four zombies. One on each side.

We were trapped.

CHAPTER TWENTY-SIX

MY MIND RACED. There had to be a way out. Together, the zombies stepped forward and the space between us shrank. I had to think quickly. If I waited too long, the gaps would close and I'd lose my chance. Suddenly, my mind jumped back to our game of run-outs and I knew what to do.

"Wait for my signal" I whispered.

Then, I ran. I burst straight for a gap between two zombies. They reacted instantly and lunged towards me. I skidded to a halt and jumped backwards. I felt a pointy finger scrape my side as it lurched.

I looked up in time to see the zombies clatter into each other where I would've been. A maelstrom of arms and legs flew into the air and tangled together. The floating ball of bone and skin hung above the ground for a second before falling to the dirt with a crack.

"NOW!" I shouted. "RUN!"

The sound of the zombies falling over seemed to wake Luca from his stupor. He and Daniel reacted quickly. They sprinted away from the two remaining zombies and jumped over the ones on the floor. I turned and ran.

Together we fled the clearing, but we had no time to waste. As I looked back, I saw all four zombies back on their feet. They raised themselves up to their fullest heights and ran after us. We set off through the woods again, hurdling logs and bending low under branches.

Behind us, the four gangly zombies tore through everything in their path. Bark and branches flew into the air as they clattered into and past the ancient trees. The ground shook as their oversized feet stomped in our wake. We were running as fast as we could, but we couldn't get away.

"This way!" Daniel shouted.

We followed him through a gap in two trees that had grown close together. As we ran further, I heard the zombies smashing into the trunks. It didn't stop them. Their heavy footsteps barely slowed down and they were soon hot on our trails again.

We reached a giant elm and used the trunk to slingshot ourselves around the corner. The footsteps slowed. The zombies hadn't seen us change direction. They moved cautiously through the trees. Their breathing was laboured, like they were gargling the air instead of swallowing it.

"Shhhh!" I gestured.

We all crouched down and carried on walking carefully away from the monsters as they prowled. If we could sneak away, we'd be safe. Finally, we were making progress. The distance between us and the zombies increased.

I turned to Daniel and smiled but, after looking back ahead, I screamed.

CHAPTER TWENTY-SEVEN

OUT OF THE darkness, a figure appeared. It was running at full speed. I just managed to brace myself as it smashed into me. I tumbled to the floor with the thing on top of me. I grabbed it by the shoulders and span around so I was on top.

It was Arj.

"Cassie!" he said, breathlessly.

"SHH!" I said, climbing off of him. We didn't have time for explanations. I pointed in the direction of the zombies and he understood. The four of us stayed perfectly still as we waited to see if they had heard the commotion.

Seconds of silence ticked by. Then, from behind the trees, the sound of heavy footsteps emerged. They grew louder and louder until they were only a few metres away.

"RUN!" I shouted again.

We sprinted back the way Arj had come and the zombies followed. We ran through the dense woodland together at full speed. However, it wasn't long until we started to spread out. Arj was slower than the rest of us and he was already out of breath. His pace dropped. I didn't notice until it was too late.

I turned around to see he had fallen. I skidded to a halt and turned back. The zombies appeared from the trees and closed in on Arj. Daniel and Luca hadn't noticed. Arj was scrambling to his feet but, in his panic, he fell again. The zombies were right behind him. Their long arms jutted awkwardly out of the darkness.

I ran as fast as I could, but they were right on top of him. Bits of spit flew from their mouths and stretched backwards across their grotesque faces. Their hunched shoulders rose and fell. Their bones clicked and creaked as they got closer.

I wasn't going to make it. Arj looked up at me with wide, terrified eyes. There was nothing I could do. A long, bony foot slammed down next to his head. Suddenly, a piercing sound erupted from the woods. It was loud and abrupt. It was a bark.

Smoke's bark.

She leapt out from behind a tree with her sharp teeth bared. The zombies jumped back in shock as Smoke landed protectively over Arj. The distraction gave me enough time to reach him. I grabbed Arj by the shoulders and hoisted him upright.

"Come on!" I said, shoving him in the right direction.

Smoke was still fending off the zombies as we made our getaway. Every time they lunged towards me or Arj, Smoke launched an assault of growls and barks until they backed off. They were confused by the dog, but it wouldn't last. We had to get away quickly. Once we'd put some distance between us and the zombies, I called Smoke to join us.

"Good girl!" I said, proudly, as she started running alongside. Her tail wagged and her tongue flopped happily out the side of her mouth as we darted through the forest once again. We ran for what seemed like hours but was probably minutes. My thighs burned and my lungs ached.

I thought we were hopelessly lost, but then I noticed something in the distance. It was a clearing like many others, but it was familiar. As we approached it, I realised I'd been there before and, at that moment, I knew exactly what to do.

CHAPTER TWENTY-EIGHT

"WE'VE BEEN HERE before!" I shouted to the group after we'd caught up with the others. "Don't you remember?"

They looked at me blankly. Sweat dripped from their faces and their chests were heaving as they searched for breath. Smoke whizzed excitedly around Daniel's legs.

"We can't stop now," Luca wheezed. "They're right behind us."

"Wait!" I said. "Trust me. Follow my lead and, when I say jump, JUMP."

Arj nodded vigorously. Daniel and Luca were more reluctant, but they didn't have a choice as the zombies were approaching fast.

"Go," I said, firmly.

We set off as the zombies smashed their way through some nearby ferns. My legs were aching, but I knew this was our only chance. I pushed forward and took the lead. Arj, Daniel and Luca were close behind. I put my head down and sprinted.

The zombies saw their opportunity as the foliage cleared and they had more space to run. Their long legs ate up the distance between us. The sound of their clicking bones grew louder. They were gaining on us.

My eyes were fixed on the ground ahead, searching for any sign that would help me. I tried to block out the sounds of heavy footsteps and focus on the task at hand. I could hear panting to either side of me.

Then, I saw it.

Just ahead, I saw the earth change.

"On my mark!" I yelled.

A few more steps and we'd be there. My breath was short and every bone in my body seared with pain.

"JUMP!" I screamed.

I swooped Smoke off the floor, planted my foot and leapt as high and as far as I could. To my right, I saw Daniel follow my lead. To my left, Luca. We landed with a deafening crash and rolled head over heels into the brambles. The dirt scratched at my skin as we slid to a sudden stop.

I looked around. Daniel and Luca were laying on their backs, breathless but unhurt. That's when I realised Arj wasn't with us. He'd fallen behind. I looked up to see him running frantically in front of the zombies. They could almost reach out and touch him and they were gaining fast. I looked at his shoulders. He was tensing up. His face was contorted and his arms were rigid.

"ARJ! RELAX!" I shouted.

He looked at me as he ran. Then, his shoulders dropped. The tension in his body fell away and his speed increased. The gap between him and the zombies opened up as he sprang high into the air and thudded down next to us. I smiled as Daniel and Luca looked on with amazement.

Then, in unison, we turned back to the zombies. They were just a few metres away from us and running at full speed. Their pointy knees clacked and cracked as they moved. Their dead eyes and pale faces almost seemed to smile as they saw us laying on the ground. Easy prey.

Then, they ran where we'd jumped.

Their skinny feet plummeted into the deep, gooey mud and their stretched bodies were flung forward with a splat. They landed face-first into the bog. All four zombies squished into the soft, gelatinous swamp. They writhed and wriggled, fiercely trying to free themselves, but it was no use. Slowly, their huge, monstrous bodies started to sink. The mud rose above their shoulders and pinned their arms to the side. They twisted and turned in a desperate attempt to escape, but their efforts were futile. The brown and black goo infiltrated their mouths and seeped into their eyes. Eventually, they were fully consumed by the bog and there was nothing left.

It was over. The zombies had sunk deep into the swamp and the woods were quiet as we stared at the empty space in front of us. A single bubble burst on the surface.

"Sick!" Daniel mumbled.

We made our way out of the woods. Luca and Arj walked home together, telling jokes and laughing the whole way. When my brother and I got back, Daniel played games on his laptop and I lounged around reading a puzzle book. Mum worked busily away in the kitchen trying to get the stains out of our clothes. She'd been annoyed with us at first, but she calmed down when we said we'd fallen over while walking Smoke. A white lie.

Dad had been working on his car since they'd returned from their meal with the Millers. The smell of roast chicken mixed with soap suds and engine oil and lingered in the air. The sun was setting slowly and filled the living room with pinks and purples. Mum was singing gently to herself as Dad came through the door.

"You know," he said, wringing his hands clean with a mucky rag. "Maybe we were too harsh on you before."

I looked up from my crossword. Daniel paused his game.

"Maybe," he continued, "we could all go for a camping trip together in Dead Man's Woods. What do you say?"

More SCARETOWN books available now.

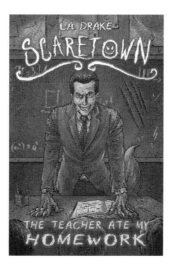

Jack and Ellie Ferguson are just trying to fit in on their first day at a new school, but life becomes more complicated when their teachers aren't quite as nice as they first appear. Now, Jack and Ellie must fight to save themselves and their new classmates from the horrors that prowl the hallways.

THE TEACHER ATE MY HOMEWORK is a creepy, thrilling and fun tale guaranteed to excite and petrify in equal measure.

AVAILABLE TO BUY NOW ON AMAZON OR READ FOR FREE ON KINDLE UNLIMITED.

More SCARETOWN books available now.

Theo and Eddie Jensen think they've found the perfect game to play after school, but things change when they are tricked by a teacher and become stuck in the VR world. Now, they must hurry to find a way back to real life before the switch is made permanent and they're trapped in virtual reality forever.

VR NIGHTMARE is a riot of extreme fun and awesome adventure packed from start to finish with screams, laughs and gasps.

AVAILABLE TO BUY NOW ON AMAZON OR READ FOR FREE ON KINDLE UNLIMITED.

VR NIGHTMARE

1.

The first day back at school after the summer holidays was always tough, but this one was going to be the toughest yet. The last traces of sunny weather had already disappeared and I trudged through the spitting rain with my little brother, Eddie. He had his heavy winter coat zipped up tight.

"That's a bit extreme isn't it, Ed?" I asked, nodding at his fur-lined hood. "You look like an Eskimo."

He scowled at me through a small gap in the fabric.

"It's supposed to be summer, Theo," he said. "Why isn't it summer?"

Eddie was always the dramatic one. I laughed and walked ahead. In truth, I was quite excited about being back at school. I'd heard the science block was being renovated and they were installing loads more computers in the IT lab. My laptop was so old, I swear I could hear it groan every time I lifted the lid. It would be great to see what new tech the school had for us to use.

As we entered the school grounds, it was obvious the building work was only just finished. There were workers still milling around and tidying up. I rushed over to a half-full skip and peered inside as a man in a hi-vis jacket chucked an old computer keyboard into it.

"Look at all this cool stuff!" I said, turning to Eddie.

"Yeah, really amazing…" he said, sarcastically. He lifted a broken mouse and let it drop back down into the skip.

I reached forward to grasp a bit of discarded motherboard but, as my fingertip grazed the edge, I heard a loud voice shout from behind me.

"Theodore Jensen!" I jumped and spun around to see my maths teacher, Mrs Quinn, staring right at me. Her old, wrinkled face was scrunched up as if she'd smelled something awful. "What do you thinking you're doing?"

"I was just…" I stumbled over my words. I could feel the faces of dozens of kids turning to stare. The heat started to rise in my cheeks.

"We were just looking at the skip," Ed said, calmly.

"Don't take that tone with me, young man," Mrs Quinn spat. "I don't recall asking *you* anything."

"We're just on our way to class," I interrupted. I knew Eddie was about to say something he'd regret.

"Well, hurry up about it," she shot back. "If I see you two around here again, you'll be serving detention for the rest of the week."

"Well, that was fun," I mumbled, as we walked briskly away from Mrs Quinn.

"You'd think the summer holidays would've mellowed her out a bit," Eddie replied.

As we turned the corner, I saw Mr Finch, the IT teacher, talking to a workman. Mr Finch was even older than Mrs Quinn, but they couldn't be more different. I caught his eye and waved from a distance. His soft face contorted happily as he threw up a hand and beckoned me over.

"Mrs Quinn told us to get to class…" Eddie whispered under his breath as we made our way to Mr Finch.

"We'll be two minutes," I said. "Don't worry."

Mr Finch finished his conversation with the workman and turned to greet us. His messy grey hair flopped back and forth in the wind.

"Hello, boys!" he said, warmly. "Have a good summer, I hope? Shame the weather's turned so quickly."

"Tell me about it!" Eddie said, pulling his hood even further over his head.

"What are the new computers like?" I asked, eagerly.

"Marvellous, Theo. Simply marvellous!" His grey-blue eyes twinkled with delight. "It's amazing how far technology has come, isn't it?"

"Can we come and play on the computers at lunch?" Eddie asked. I nudged him in the ribs for being rude, but I also looked to Mr Finch for an answer.

"I'd like nothing more!" he said, beaming again. "I tell you what, I'll rustle up some snacks and show you all the new gizmos."

"That sounds great," I said, sincerely. Even Eddie looked excited.

"But," Mr Finch said, looking suddenly at his wristwatch. "Shouldn't you two be getting to class? It's gone nine."

He was right. We were late. We were so busy talking that we hadn't noticed everyone leave. The courtyard was completely empty. We thanked Mr Finch and turned to go. We ran back the way we'd come. I was still smiling at the thought of playing on the new computers at lunch when we turned the corner and crashed right into someone coming the other way.

My face smooshed into a broad stomach. A button poked me in the eye as Eddie clattered into the back of me and, together, we were thrust further into a mass of flesh and fabric before being rebounded and landing flat on our backs. In a haze, I looked up to see the snarling face of Mrs Quinn.

VR NIGHTMARE is available now. Read the whole book for free on Kindle Unlimited or purchase online. Visit www.scaretownbooks.com for more information.

Join the conversation at
www.twitter.com/scaretownbooks